PLIGHT OF THE SYRENNI

LORIN PETRAZILKA

FATEBOUND BOOKS
A WOMEN-OWNED IMPRINT

The content of this book is protected under Federal Copyright Laws. Any unauthorized use of this material is prohibited. No portion of this book may be reproduced in any form without express written permission from the author.

Plight of the Syrenni
First Edition
Copyright 2020 Lorin Z Pillai

All Rights Reserved. Printed in the United States of America.

Published by Fatebound Books
For rights inquires, please contact rights@fateboundbooks.com

FATEBOUND BOOKS

ISBN 978-1-7360622-5-8 (hardcover)
ISBN 978-1-7360622-2-7 (paperback)
ISBN 978-1-7360622-3-4(e-book)

Cover design by Alberto Carranza and Lorin Z Pillai

This is a work of fiction. Names, characters, places, and incidents either are the products of the author's imagination or are used fictitiously. Any resemblance to actual persons, living or dead, businesses, events, companies or locales are entirely coincidence.

TABLE OF CONTENTS

CHAPTER 1

The smooth, cool metal of my ancient crest, worn almost flat from years of rubbing, comforted me as I slid my thin webbed fingers over its surface. After countless cycles of its possession by the first born female of the Syrenni Azal familia line, the detailed relief carved into it had all but leveled out. Much of the embossing I recalled from when I had peered at it in my maeder's hands had nearly vanished, much like my memories of her. But I couldn't help myself. I turned to the relic when I needed solace, or when I was about to do something stupid. I rubbed it far more frequently lately.

I had taken it out from its lucky hiding spot, a carefully chosen nook under a sheet of rock in my watery Syran bedroom. To call it a bedroom was generous, it was merely a dank cave in the lowest area of the Lacausia Palace. It was a lucky alcove, because only my Syrenni fingers could feel and pick up the perfectly fitted slick rock that covered the small compartment, under my submerged sleeping board. The Umorfae, if they ever bothered to look, would probably not even be able to see or feel the joint where the two stones met, once it was closed.

"Naiya!" My sister exclaimed as she rushed in, her back fins billowed behind her. My twin in every respect except one: her clouded eyes. "Put that away before you are caught with it!"

As if on cue, the summoning bell clanged angrily.

"Well, that is that, I suppose," I said to Neila, then ducked under the water and swam below the board, to put the precious sigil back in place. Inner workings of the disc shifted inside it as I rotated it in my palm, yet they were inert. I wished I could remember how to activate the weighty, flattened sphere as I placed it in the nook. The Taming had washed that knowledge away. The heavy rock piece grated against the surface as I slid it over to close it, reverberating up my nimble fingers and through my arms. Relief surged as it finally clunked into place. Holding the relic rooted me to what my people once were, but hiding it again gave me the sense that this one piece would remain safe. It was perhaps a false sense of security.

I resurfaced and climbed out of the sunken half room just as the bell clamored its obnoxious racket again, demanding one of us Syrenni up to the actual liveable areas of the castle. It was an order to ascend and to do the bidding of whatever Umorfae was on the other end of the summoning line.

Three rings. Opius. At least it wasn't Silvanis. Opius usually only used harsh wording. Usually. Silvanis could be downright brutal—depending on his mood.

Neila gave me a small smile. "I am sorry sister, it is unfortunate Opius prefers you."

I looked up to the ceiling and took a calming breath, then let it slowly out of my gills. "Indeed," I simply responded. I smoothed my waist-length hair and rushed along the cold, stained marble floor, leaving a trail of filmy water behind me.

I walked up to the grand staircase of the great hall, Opius stood tapping his talons on the brilliant white flooring, the beautiful opal veins in the seamless landing matched his white iridescent hair. His rigidly crossed arms made his bulging muscles extrude further out. Opius's towering form was as imposing as his manner.

"I expect you to arrive faster. I need to depart and cannot be waylaid by your tardiness," he barked.

"My apologies, my Lord. How may I serve you?" I asked with my head bowed. I studied his feet, as I always did when in his presence. It was easier than trying to look up at him, as he was more than twice my height. It also allowed me to avoid how he usually glowered down at me with his intense teal eyes. His disdain for me and my kind was etched permanently on his face, though he at least was not as bad as some.

"I require a room prepared, I plan to have a visitor. A Vale Born. The Faeries sent word that one is on the way here." His claws extended slightly and raked the ground in a repetitive way that made me shudder. The sound it made against the smooth floor sent chills down my back, making my dorsal fin scrunch involuntarily.

"Shall I prepare the room for a filia, like the last one, or a filio?" I inquired without looking up.

"I do not know, the Faeries did not inform me of the gender. Those glitter rats are not dependable for complete information. There are two Vale Born left from that part of the human realm that I know of, one female, and one male, I do not know which will arrive."

...Left?

"I shall prepare for either," I answered quietly without raising my head. I dared not ask which part of the human realm he was referring to, though I wished I could. I would know how long I would have before he returned.

"Water for life," he declared as I heard a thud, no doubt his fist rapping across his broad chest.

"Water for life," I affirmed through my jagged, clenched teeth. I intoned the words, as all Umorfae subjects were expected to, though it turned my stomach to do so. To have to repeat them every day, at every interaction with any Umorfae was a depressing reminder that we held no status. But I did not want another beating, and had no time for such repercussions. So I continued to mutter the bastardized words, like a good little Syrenni whose only intent was to please her master.

I stayed still as he stomped off, waiting until I heard the massive castle door clang shut. *I have very little time.* I hurried up the curving staircase to Opius's block of rooms, an alcove of three doors on the third floor of the eastern wing. I pushed the translucent stone door open, I could barely contend with its thick rigid weight.

I entered the first door on the left, the room he frequently used for guests, or exploits. His other two rooms he kept to himself, and only had me clean them on a rare occasion.

I whirled in a cleaning frenzy around the room, which was bathed in luminous lavender light, tinted as it passed through the subtly colored, clouded quartz walls. The beautiful stone of the upper castle was a stark contrast to the dark, dingy rock of the underground structure. It was an ironic reflection of the Umorfae themselves, with their stunning outward appearance. Only by being their servant did I see through to the murky base beneath the shimmering surface.

I made quick work of the messy bed, peeling off the sheets left-over from Opius's latest conquest. Some female Umorfae courtier. He had a way of enticing most anyone. Being the Empress's cousin and Generalis of the Palace regiment certainly helped as well.

I curled my lip in disgust as I balled up the bedding, then threw fresh ones over the luxurious mattress, tucking them in around the exquisitely carved amethyst bed frame. I traced my hand over the cool stone for a moment, I was always drawn to amethyst. It sparkled and refracted inside the hard crystal, grown into existence eons before by the Petrafae.

I wondered what happened to the once great race that could make entire structures out of various stones and minerals. They had used their power over earth to create Lacausia Palace, before the Umorfae had taken over. Now their remnants were probably scraping out an existence on the fringes of Alternis.

I shook myself out of my short lived daydream, *no time for that.* I needed to hurry. I slid over to the large stone dresser and opened the quartz drawers. *Everything in this faexhole is so heavy!* I grunted as I pulled, finally getting it ajar enough to work free sets of clothing to dress either a male or female. Comfortable sleeping clothes, light and fluttery dinner attire. I placed each near the vanity. I then checked the vanity drawer for the instaura, the colors for the face to apply if it is a female. Or a male who likes to wear it. Still unused and in its expected spot, I closed the drawer and hurried out of the room.

I rushed down the stairs, so fast that I stumbled on the second to last step. I careened headfirst into an uncontrolled topple, when a muscled arm shot out from behind the alcove that was nestled under the base of the landing. It deftly scooped around my waist and redirected my forward motion into a graceful turn.

"Caught you, my love," a husky male voice said into my finned ear.

I gasped as he pulled me into a tight embrace, his large build formed around me, encasing me in an insistent hug. I wriggled free and spun around.

"Locrien!" I exclaimed in a quiet shriek. "You scared the faex out of me! What are you doing? We could get caught!"

"Let them catch us," he said as he pulled me in closer, and bent all the way down to press his forehead against mine.

I pulled my head back slightly, my nictitating membranes blinked over my eyes as I studied him. I fluttered my eyelashes and flashed him a coy smile. "Foolish Umorfae, throwing caution to the wind."

Locrien grinned broadly. "What can I say, you have made me lose all sense of propriety."

I let out a small laugh and pecked his cheek.

"Do you call that a kiss?" He asked haughtily.

"Well I-"

He drew me in and kissed me deeply, his white opal hair cascaded over his shoulder and down my back as he leaned over me. It mantled me in a shroud of silken strands. I ran my hand along his cheekbone, up to his long pointed ears. He clenched me tightly as he groaned.

He pulled back a little and whispered against my mouth, "I have told you before not to touch my ears, unless you are ready for me to rip off that frock right here."

I looked up innocently into his eyes. "I forgot, my love." I gave him a knowing smirk as he growled in response.

I pulled away as I heard footsteps down the hall. "Is there anything else you require, Praetor Locrien?" I asked somewhat loudly, hoping whoever the footsteps belonged to did not catch any of the earlier conversation, or indiscretions.

"Yes, I require you to assist me further. My quarters could use your attention."

My jaw dropped, he had never been so bold as to mention me going to his quarters, not aloud at least.

The footsteps changed direction, then gradually faded.

"You know I cannot go to your quarters now!" I hissed a whisper at him.

He merely shrugged in response. "It was worth a try, was it not?"

"Too risky. Besides, I have work to do, to prepare things for Opius."

"Relax, my love. He will be gone for some time."

"How do you know?" I asked quizzically. *Tell me.*

He leaned closer and said, "He is going to the Southwest Passage, to the tear in the Vale. He received word from a Faerie that a Vale Born had entered. It will be some time before he or she is through to our side. He wanted to be there in time to greet the Fae hybrid as it entered Alternis, and then bring it here to the palace."

"For what purpose?"

"I do not know," he answered slowly, as he curled a lock of my hair in his thick fingers.

Damnatus. At least now I know how far he is going. Southwest Passage. That gives me half a rotation at least before he returns.

"I must go and see to what Opius ordered me to do. But, after I have served the nocte fare meal, I will find you. Water for li-"

"Do not say the words, never affirm to me. I will not ever ask it of you." He wrapped me in a tight embrace.

I squeezed my eyes shut, a pang of conflicting emotions washed over me. *Why is he the only Umorfae like this? Why must all others enforce submission?* I gave him one last quick kiss.

I let go and made to leave, he grabbed for me, to try and demand more. I shuffled aside and evaded him. I admonished him with a glance, then quirked a sultry smile at him, before I turned away.

I swished my hips as I walked quickly to the servant laundry, knowing he was watching my every move.

I descended into the hallway for the laundry, which was on the way to my quarters. I neared the entrance to the large wash room, then passed it.

The one saving grace of living in the basement, with the various water pits and tunnels, was the nearly endless lengths of waterways to explore.

I passed a few more openings, before making a right turn then descended again, into the open pipes. A set of stairs lowered into the dark, murky water that ran under the castle. Under, and through, to the outside.

I stepped in, and slipped below, to traverse the castle water-ways. All the way to the exit which I had forced open.

CHAPTER 2

I felt as close to what I imagined the Untamed Syrenni felt, as I swam through the waterway at a rapid speed. If a being were to stand near the edge to watch me pass, they may not even register I had come and gone. Before the Taming, we Syrenni were nearly unstoppable once submerged in the water. For eons we had lived as a free people, many endeavored to trap and control us. It was not until Empress Delphine, the grandmaeder of the current Umorfae Empress, managed to capture our beloved leader. Their line of queens made a habit of collecting the female rulers of other lands.

Perhaps one day we would have a new leader, one that could restore us to our rightful place in Alternis. I thought with reverence of our lost Queen Sereia as my fins fluttered, and my feet kicked in a whir. Having both fins and legs gave me the advantage of being amphibious. Though slower on land, my unchecked speed in the water was nothing short of stunning.

My protective, thin membranes covered my eyes in a transparent milky lens, allowing me to see while swimming. The particles in the volume streaked past as I propelled forward.

I must hurry, I do not have much time. Turn after turn through the memorized waterways, I pushed on.

My eyes had adjusted to the near blackness so that I could see just enough of what surrounded me, I knew I was nearing the grated opening that I had broken through previously. Intended to let water out but keep the Syrenni contained within the confines of the wretched castle, the Umorfae had not realized I had managed to finally compromise it. It took many rotations of short visits to the site, working it open more and more until I could finally wriggle through.

As I exited the final aperture, the normally soft exterior light was so bright, it felt like an attack on my senses. I shot out of the opening and arced down into the open, natural river below. It always took me a few moments to allow my vision to adjust. I had no time to wait for it this time. I flurried along on recall alone, trusting that I had practiced the run enough times that I would not hit any rocks that obstructed the way.

I curved left, then quickly banked right, avoiding two rocky outcroppings that I remembered. I sailed past the jutting obstructions, then deftly avoided three more in my path. Just as my vision began to filter back in, my shoulder clipped the edge of a mass, pitting me in an uncontrolled spin and sending my careening off course.

I realized too late that I had forgotten the last obstacle. A small jetty that crept in from the edge like a jagged finger.

I tucked my head down to avoid crashing face first, then slammed into the sand bar that bordered the waterway. My hips flipped over my upper body, and smacked down on the narrow beach. I gasped for air from the sudden impact, the wind blown from both my mouth and gills. I lay stunned for a few moments, trying to regain my breath.

After a few strained breaths, I managed to stabilize myself. I rubbed my injuries and looked them over quickly, a few missing scales and probably some sore muscles later, *not too bad. I don't have time for tending them, though. I must press on.*

I rolled back over and slid myself off the shore, then ducked under the water and swam as fast as I could. I could not let the injury to my finely plated skin slow me down. I had to get to my meeting point. The Ignisfae I needed to rendezvous with would not stay long. And now, finally, I had news that could help us both.

CHAPTER 3

Onward I pressed, staying dangerously low to the riverbed floor. It was a lesser risk than being near the surface, as disturbing the water might catch the attention of an Umorfae soldier, if one happened to be nearby. It could mean death for me or one of my kind, if the soldier managed to make it back to Lacausia Palace and alert the others. They would no doubt find how I had escaped, and fix the tunnel's exit. And if a soldier were nearby, I would not be able to fight them. The Taming had robbed me of the ability to rip any foe to shreds with my teeth. Beautiful lips hiding a deadly weapon, we used to say. My three rows of barbed teeth were only good for eating standard meals at this point. No, a few belly scrapes was a better alternative.

I neared the border of Lacausia, the river diminished to a slight stream. I would have to continue on foot soon, there was not enough volume in the brook to move safely through it. I surfaced silently, allowing only the upper part of my large eyes to crest the water. I spun in place, quickly scanning the area.

Nothing.

The Praegra Forest hummed in the distance. I was to meet the Ignisfae at the juncture of the two lands, where rocky Lacausia melded with the trees. He dare not risk going any further south, if he were caught by an Umorfae they would drown him on sight, with an orb of water forced around his head until life was strangled out of him. The irony of their saying 'Water for life' was not lost on me, they often used the affirmation as a threat. It was their method of warning against any action by another race of Fae or lower being, if that action could be viewed as a disturbance by the Fae that control the liquid element. Water for life, until they used it to dole out death.

I deemed the area free from the water manipulators, and slowly emerged from the stream. I crept to the bank, and moved quietly through, allowing my longer rear frills to hang behind me to erase my footprints as I walked along.

Quarter rotation, my innate inner clock told me. I need to give him my information, then head back quickly. *Hopefully he is here.*

We met here every seven rotations. I continued coming, in the hopes that helping him would help me, and my people. Somehow, some way, we needed to break the cycle of Umorfae rule. They presided over us ruthlessly, and kept the other races of Fae in submissive check.

I rounded a bend and saw him, partially obstructed by the outermost tree of the Praegra Forest. Wrapped in a traditional Ignisfae dhoti, the long continuous piece of woven tan fabric showed off his build. He shifted slightly, the wrap rippled a little from his hardened chest muscles. I followed the curve of the cloth up, where it continued coiling around to cover his face. His sharp eyes assessed me quickly, his gaze darted around to see if anyone else was with me.

He emerged and anchored his spear in the ground, and waited

for me to approach.

"Greetings Syrenni," his rich voice intoned.

"Salvé, Ignisfae."

We never used names, I had never even seen his face. I had only glimpsed his cognac eyes that danced with fire, a sliver of his dark glistening skin, and a wisp of his black and ruby hair.

I cleared my throat. "I bring news, important news. I must tell you quickly and then depart. Opius will return in perhaps a quarter rotation, I will need to be back before then."

The flames in his eyes flashed as I told him of the Vale Born that was soon to arrive, and Opius's plan to bring him or her to the palace.

"We have a rare opportunity, Syrenni. We must strike while we can, but in a careful way. Return here on the next rotation, but you will need more time before you will be able to go back to the castle. Perhaps an extra quarter rotation. Will you do it?"

My membranes blinked reflexively over my eyes, the risk I would be taking to return again so quickly caused my body to shrink back in fear. Though, I must take this chance.

"Yes, I will do it." *I cannot be afraid, I must do this.*

"Magna, I will see you in one rotation. I will have another Fae with me. I will tell you more at that time. Burn brightly, Syrenni."

He turned, then sprinted away. I watched him for a moment, as his powerful legs propelled him across the land. Though the Ignisfae were the same size on average to an Umorfae, his height did not scare me. He could have been menacing, rip me to shreds with his canines or eviscerate me with his weapons, though I had no fear of him. There was something about him, his character, which spoke to my inner soul. It silently soothed and promised that he would not ever use his hulking size or power against me. Ever.

As he disappeared from view I realized I had wasted time, allowing my mind to wander a moment. I turned and hurried to return to the stream, to my prison of Lacausia Palace beyond.

CHAPTER 4

I slipped back in through the broken grate, then moved quickly through the network of dark tunnels in the bowels of the palace.

I lifted my head slowly from the water, ready to carefully emerge and go about my duties as if I had never even been away. The musty, putrid smells of the underground structure filled my nasal passages. I nearly wretched from it. Being outside, even just for a little bit, cleaned the stench from me.

"You risk much by your intrigues, Naiya," a meek female voice whispered behind me.

I spun quickly to see my sister, who had been hiding in a dark corner of the last tunnel, before the exit near our quarters.

"Neila," I began. No, I could not tell her anything. If she had any knowledge of what I was doing, she would be in danger. And if I was caught, they would punish her as well. "I know I should not explore the tunnels, but my heart yearns to be free. I have only gone a few times."

She only looked back at me, with those dull, defeated eyes. At last she said, "That is not the only intrigue I mean. Just...be more careful."

I opened my mouth to say something, to make something up.

I had never told her about Locrien, about any of it. But somehow, she knew. I snapped my mouth shut instead. Silence was better than lies.

The Taming had differing degrees of success. Neila was one who was completely Tamed. She always did as she was told, and never balked at our current lot in life. But there were a few who were not Tamed so easily. They retained a thread of knowledge that was supposedly wiped out. That thread was a risk and a liability, but so precious that it needed to be protected. Sheltered and hidden for the time that the Syrenni someday break their bonds and swim free once again. *Neila must never know that I carry the thread.*

"I should return to work, before Opius returns. Have you seen him?" I asked, hoping she would stop staring at me with that hollow gaze. I kept my breathing as steady as I could, trying to not let on how much I had actually swam.

"No, I do not think he has returned," she answered as I climbed out of the waterway.

"Let us go to the laundry, and complete the work before he does," I said, without giving her another glance. I walked out of the chamber, and heard her light footfalls swish on the ground behind me.

We worked in silence, washing, scrubbing, wringing. Our fingers worked quickly to eradicate the stains left behind on the fabrics they carelessly used. I scrubbed harder than necessary. Washing their clothing and bedding made me feel as if I could somehow wash the Umorfae off of me. Their imprint, their breath that seemed to cling to my skin, their meaty handgrip on our lives. As I cleaned with fury, Locrien flashed in my mind. His scent, his comforting presence. He was different. But he was also a means to an end.

The summoning bell erupted in harsh strokes and cut through the silence like a knife jabbed through flesh, startling me so badly I jumped.

Four bells. Silvanis.

My blood went cold, colder than it usually was. Silvanis was the most treacherous of all, half the time his requests were malicious, and not out of any direct need that he had, but rather to remind whoever served him that he was in control of their lives. He took wicked delight in tormenting the Syrenni. Even though Opius was of higher rank than he, no one ever balked at his treatment of us.

Neila's membranes flashed twice over her eyes in fear, her body cowered smaller and smaller as she realized who called.

I stood a little taller, and gave her a reassuring touch to her slim shoulder. "I will go, I can handle him."

She quaked, her black, almond-shaped eyes becoming almost round. "No, no. I should go, Naiya."

"No, Neila, I can make something up as to why you could not answer the summons, if he asks. I will go. He is harder on you."

I turned to head up to the main palace without waiting for her to agree. I knew, she was too scared. She would say no again to my offer to go in her place, even if she was too terrified to willingly go to him. Whatever he wanted, hopefully it didn't take too long. And if there was punishment involved, I prayed it didn't impede my swimming ability. I would need every bit of speed I could muster when I left for the meeting place again.

I rushed up the stairs, hoping a quicker arrival to his summons would lessen any preloaded annoyance he had.

I scurried around the bend from the hall that descended into the dank servant level, and ran smack into a wall of muscle.

19

CHAPTER 5

I stumbled backward, my vision sparkling from the sudden force. Just as quickly as I fell back, a massive hand clamped down on my shoulder and pulled me forward. The same shoulder I had injured during my last rendezvous.

I winced in pain at the force exuded on my sensitive skin, then looked up to see who had caught me.

I went still as Silvanis's cold blue eyes returned a harsh glare down at me. He pulled his hand away and eyed the missing scales, some of which stuck to his broad palm. He sneered and wiped it on his muted teal leather breeches, a few of the iridescent flakes fluttered to the ground. I tried not to panic as I realized I had no explanation for the injury.

"Praetor Locrien getting too rough with you?" he asked with a smirk.

My eyes widened ever so slightly, but I schooled my face into neutral submission. "I scuffed it picking something up from under the laundress table."

"I never knew laundry to be such an accident prone task." His words practically slithered between his gritted teeth and curled lip.

He knows he knows he knows.

"How may I serve you, my Lord?" I asked as I looked down, desperate to avoid any further comments.

"My talons require sharpening."

My body wanted to wretch, it took all of my effort to keep my breathing even and prevent myself from emptying whatever might be in my stomach on the gleaming marble floor. Sharpening any of their talons was considered the worst task of all. The job not only reminded us of what they could do with their threatening claws, but also of our position, grovelling at their feet and doing their bidding.

"Of course, my Lord, I will follow you to the balneo."

He turned on his heel and stomped to the nearest bathing room, I walked behind him as quickly as I could. His long strides made it difficult for me to keep up.

He strode into the wide chamber, its large open archways framed the raised pedestals used for polishing their feet. They loomed over the Syrenni even without the extra elevation.

Silvanis roughly sat down on one of the upholstered seats, its tufted cushion squeaked under his weight. He thumped a foot onto the elevated polishing platform, and tapped his claws against the smooth marble, making a tinking sound that grated at my delicate ears. I looked around, no one else was in the balneo, the bays adjacent to the pedicure area were vacant. Those were used to wash and style hair, or to rub essential oils into their opalescent white skin. But never to cut hair. Only Fae who had committed a serious wrongdoing had their hair forcibly cut, and with how slowly Fae hair grew, it would be many cycles until evidence of a past error couldn't be seen. I wondered how the Syrenni that specialized in Umorfae hair and skin care did not ever attempt to cut a braid, or slit a throat or two while they had one of them prostrate in the lounge chairs. Just a rapid slice, and their cerulean blue blood would come brimming out. The Umorfae certainly deserved either, or both.

I looked back to find Silvanis staring down at me impatiently. I willed my face into a glazed, placid demeanor, and hoped he would not catch on to my momentary murderous daydream. I averted my eyes and focused instead on the set of rasps and polishing accoutrements, all laid neatly out next to the platform. I did not look back up as I worked, and attempted to keep my breathing steady as I honed and buffed his talons into even sharper weapons. I could feel his sneer as he watched me work, the disdain emanated from him like an oozing, festering wound.

I blotted out what I felt from him, instead I kept myself where I should be—or at least where he thought I should be—with my knees on the hard ground as he sat in comfort above me.

A clang from the fortress entrance startled me from my intent focus. I looked up at Silvanis, who had stilled, his gaze locked toward the sound. A small sliver of the main staircase was visible from our location in the balneo, just enough to see whoever it was pass by.

Opius crossed the narrow view, followed by a female. A beautiful, strange female, her pale golden hair tied back in a rudimentary braid. And her clothing, that was the most unusual part. No sheen or shimmer to the fabrics, a blocky cut shirt, and tight fitting pants. Not the kind of garments one would see in Alternis.

It was the Vale Born whom he sought, he had found her and brought her back as planned. My eyes softened a little, ever so slightly as I beheld her, thinking of the last Vale Born that had come to Lacausia Palace. Opius had whisked her away somewhere, to where, I never did find out.

Silvanis shot to his feet. "The Generalis has returned, you are dismissed," he said with a hard-edged tone. Opius glanced over to us before disappearing from sight, leading the female by the arm. She hadn't so much as looked in our direction, as she appeared to be busy marvelling at the castle.

I realized, with great relief, that him seeing me attending Silvanis would most likely nullify any questions in his mind. My escape to rendezvous with the Ignisfae could hopefully be easily explained away by Silvanis's demands. I turned my head to find him already storming off, then got up off the floor.

My legs ached from being upon the stone for so long. I briefly stretched, before turning to head back down to the servant quarters. Exhaustion was settling in, the significant effort it took to swim the distance to the meeting place, combined with the fear-laced encounter with Silvanis, had left me feeling depleted. Hopefully I could disappear for some time down below and steal some rest.

I had barely closed my eyes, when the summoning bell rang three times. Opius was demanding my assistance yet again. No doubt to help him woo the unwitting female he had procured from the Southwest Tear. I slid off my sleeping platform and trudged out of the confined, dank room.

As I emerged from the servant barracks, the bright diffuse light of the castle made me cringe. It always took me some time to adjust to the extreme disparity between the two. I held the heel of my hand to my temple to massage the immediate headache it gave me.

A form to my right swept in and corralled me before I realized what was happening.

"You should pay closer attention to what may be lurking in the corners!" a voice taunted in my ear.

I caught my breath as I realized it was Locrien, lying in wait for me yet again. I quickly looked around to see if anyone was in the area. This part of the castle was always a low traffic area fortunately. "Faex, Locrien! Stop scaring me!"

A broad, toothy smile spread across his face. "I can think of better things that you can do with your mouth besides cursing." He waggled his eyebrows suggestively as he angled his face down to mine.

I finally laughed, the tightness I held inside me unfurling a bit. I smiled and shook my head at him. "You never stop, do you." Not a question. But I had to admit, I enjoyed how he had a habit of doing this, even if it put us at risk. My life was so devoid of anything lighthearted, our little intrigue—you could even call it a relationship—gave me at least a piece of something to cling to. Even if I did have ulterior motives. I pushed that thought aside, I didn't want to think about the ways I used him.

I leaned in and kissed him, deeply—just for a moment—before I pushed off of him and settled my garment in place. "I need to attend to Opius and his guest, I believe they will be needing a meal served shortly."

"And, after? Will you come to my quarters, as promised?"

I hesitated, such a dangerous game we played. I needed to be able to depart directly after serving the Mare Fare meal to meet up with the Ignisfae, and I needed to have the energy to make the swim as fast as I could in both directions. Losing sleep with Locrien probably wasn't the wisest thing to do. Finally I batted my eyes up at him. "Yes, I will."

He gave me a wolfish grin as I swept wordlessly away, toward the staircase which ascended to Opius's block of rooms. I didn't dare turn around to see the lust that was no doubt in his eyes, as he waited before walking away.

CHAPTER 6

Opius appeared outside his rooms as I arrived.

"The Vale Born, Lily, is inside bathing now. Collect her discarded clothing and leave something for her to wear to nocte fare. Something…revealing."

I tried not to shudder at the curl of his lip. Instead, I lowered my head with a subjugated nod, then silently entered the room.

She bathed with her back to the door, lounging in the large amethyst bathtub. Her dirty, mud-caked garments were strewn about the floor. Some of the crust had flaked off onto the polished marble stone, marring the otherwise impeccable room. I gathered up her things quietly and whisked the dirt into a receptacle. I carefully laid out a feminine set for her, fluttery light fabrics that would fit Opius's request. She never even turned as I completed my work, before I exited the room.

He was waiting again as I came out. "Go prepare our meal now. Make sure we are not bothered by anyone. Also, be sure to serve both vinisohm and vocafortis."

My eyes widened slightly at the demand. The combination of the two alcohols could be intense. "Of course, Generalis. It will be done," I said without looking up.

He had plied the last Vale Born with both, also. I didn't know what had happened, after her visit to the castle. She had spent several rotations here, and then accompanied Opius on an outing. Had he returned her to the tear in the Vale which she came from? I never found out. I wondered, did he ever feel bad about seducing female after female? Was it the fact that Vale Born were Fae hybrids, and therefore something different and enticing? I supposed I was no better given what I was doing with Locrien. At least with Opius it seemed to be just your average sexual conquest, my drive went much deeper, and darker. I was doing something far worse. Yet my actions were a result of our enslavement, and I liked to imagine a world where I wouldn't be driven to seduce a male for information.

I attempted to push aside my black thoughts as I descended the stairs toward the culina, to begin the meal preparation.

I worked quickly, alongside the Syrenni that focused their efforts on cooking. It was against our nature to be in the kitchen. Among our race, the males did the cooking and cleaning. Perhaps it was another way the Umorfae delighted in dominating us, by forcing us into roles that were not natural. Yet one more reminder; it did not matter what we wanted, or what we were comfortable with, they would designate it for my sisterhood. And the males—the few of them that existed—were used solely for breeding stock, to keep the number of servants at an acceptable number. But not too many, lest we outnumber the Umorfae. The final disheartening stab at the Syrenni that our keepers enjoyed was eating our unfertilized eggs for mane fare every rotation. And not only that, we had to cook our precious eggs for them, then serve them.

The thoughts of my race's existence roiled in my head as I prepared platters of food. My hunger tugged at me as I loaded up a delicacy that I would enjoy devouring. Shell meats, piled high in an intricate pyramid. I shook my head at the thought, and continued to arrange everything to Opius's pleasing.

I delivered each tray in stages to the front dining room. I finally saw the female, Lily, up close. She was seated with Opius, who was busy peppering her with questions about her life in the human realm. Was this how he managed to bed so many females? By showing such intense interest in their lives? He barraged her with continuous questions about how many siblings she had, what she did with her time, what skills she possessed. I started to see his pattern; pour a drink, ask another question. My nerves fluttered at the way she peered at me curiously as I delivered each tray, she kept attempting to make eye contact. I feared she would call too much attention to me, and Opius might notice the damage to my scales. He had seen me with Silvanis and might pass it off as something he had done. However, I didn't need him musing over what had transpired. I would have to continue on with the deception about hurting myself doing laundry. *Laundry* of all things. *Why didn't I come up with a better lie at the time?*

I exited the room to return to the nearby servants nook, once they had left I could clean their final plates and be done. Fortunately there was a low stool I could rest on while I waited for them to finish their meal. I slumped over on the hard stool, beyond tired by the time they were done and practically dead on my feet as I rose up to clear their remnants from the table.

Opius and Lily's footsteps past the nook startled me out of my momentary reprieve. I peered around the corner to see them disappear into the darkened sitting room, the half full bottle of vinisohm swung from Opius's hand.

I breathed a sigh, at least now I could clean up after them and dismiss myself. This was the typical point where he would want privacy with his guest. I hurried into the dining room and collected the used plates, then piled them on the tray before I rushed to the culina. I smiled as Ondri came into view, dusted in flour from preparing the dough for the next rotation. She had been there after my maeder passed, had been the one that lessened the hurt and guided Neila and I through our growing cycles.

I set the tray next to two dull-eyed Syrenni that tended the wash bins, still hard at work. I washed with them, as tired as I was, I did not want to increase their burden. Ondri walked over, then rubbed my shoulders as I continued cleaning.

"You are so tense, my filia! And...are you missing scales? Who has hurt you?" She turned me to face her, inspecting me all over.

"No one, Maeder Ondri, I just had a little accident. That is all."

Her membranes blinked, as she narrowed her eyes and nodded. "I see."

Something about her response made me want to shield myself, like she could sense that the injury was from something I should not have been doing. That perhaps it was something she herself had done before. And nothing got by her.

I finished washing, then set the dishes aside to dry. "I should get some rest, Maeder Ondri."

"Of course, my filia."

It would have been smarter to return to my quarters and sleep. Risk was my most frequent companion of late. I didn't bother to rap on his door as I arrived, and slid open the stone wall to his barrack enough that I could slip in. The darkened room was empty except for a bed, big enough for one Umorfae. I could distinguish his sizable profile sitting on the mattress, waiting for me to arrive. I closed the door, making sure not to make too much sound.

"Praetor Locrien, you have need of me?" I had to be careful, I didn't want to be caught being overly familiar and uncouth.

He rushed and scooped me up, I had nearly forgotten how fast his kind could be. There was not even time for my membranes to blink before he had swept me into his arms. I gasped a breath as he swung me around, then buried his face in my neck.

"I am so glad you have finally come. I was getting to the point of wanting to hunt you down!"

I had gotten to know his voice, his tone was lighter than other Umorfae, it carried a gentleness that the others lacked. I smiled as he spun me slowly in the deep embrace. He walked to the bed as he pulled his face away to peer at me. His profile was barely visible in the low light, but I could make out the strong jaw and the fine, straight bridge of his nose. He slipped off my garment, then lowered me down and began to hoist himself over me. As Locrien bent closer to kiss me, I held up my hand to his cheek. "I want to be on top this time," I whispered as I slid my hand up to his ear. He clenched his fists in the sheets as he stifled a groan. I slipped out from under him and we switched positions in a flash. I eased myself onto him, he filled me so completely that I arched my back in response. His hands along my side encompassed the entire length of my hips, as he pulled me in a steadily increasing rhythm.

I lost myself in those moments, the stolen time that I should have been sleeping and he should have been guarding. But we took it anyway, and basked in the small joy. Release thundered through me as he sat up, taking each breast into his mouth, one at a time.

He released the tips, then gritted his teeth and clamped down on my lower back, and erupted into me.

I panted in short bursts, unsuccessful attempts at catching my breath. His chest heaved as he flopped backward onto the bed. I leaned over him and dragged my lips along his broad chest. He was still breathing hard when he gasped my name. I placed my fingers to his mouth to quiet him, and to feel his full lips against my fingerpads.

"I should go, though I wish I could stay," I said quietly. My heart sank at the thought of what I kept from him. Things had become so complicated, I had allowed this to go too far.

"Will I see you on the next rotation?"

Guilt tugged as I hesitated a moment. "I will try." I didn't allow another word as I slid the door open, then slipped out.

CHAPTER 7

I awoke to the summoning bell, the first round had startled me, but I didn't hear the number, was it three or four? It was rarely two, Empress Celestine's children had their own handmaidens. And never one, the Empress had her own servants available at all times. Nevertheless, one and two bells were reserved for them throughout the entire palace. I waited on my bed for the second chorus to indicate who required me to attend them.

I breathed a sigh as it rang three times. I slipped into the water then swam for the edge as relief washed over me. Opius would be distracted by his guest, it was most likely just food requirements and perhaps some light cleaning. As I started climbing out I realized I was fairly sore from the night before, and winced at my leg muscles that had been pushed to their limit. I could not hide a private smile to myself, my time with Locrien had been glorious. It was foolish, though. I would need all the strength I could muster to accomplish the task later with the Ignisfae.

Requiring a bit more effort than usual, I dashed up the stairs to the rooms and found Opius waiting at the top. He wordlessly motioned to the guest room, I bowed my head and entered.

The Vale Born, Lily, was still asleep. I paused a moment while

I took in her appearance. She looked so peaceful, so lovely. Her pale gold hair tucked behind her pointed ear was like silken flax. Such a strange and unique color, prior to the other Vale Born, I had only ever seen the silver-black hair of the Syrenni, the opal of the Umorfae, and the wisp of black and ruby Ignisfae. I wondered as I gazed at her, what was the world she was from like? As no creature from our realm could enter there—save for the Faeries—I would never know first hand. I shook my head and returned my focus to the task at hand. I cleaned and laid out clothes without making a sound. When I exited, Opius still waited by his main room. He hissed a whisper, "Prepare mane fare for two and deliver it to my study table." He did not wait for me to confirm, before he turned to enter his office.

I was relieved to have limited interaction, I feared I would give myself away if I had to be in his presence for too long. I went to the culina to prepare the trays. A familiar sight at the cook fire greeted me. "Bonum mane, Maeder Ondri," I said as I entered.

She gave me a weak smile and waved with her utensil, then brushed her formerly black hair—now grey as she approached the Fading—out of her aged face. I returned the smile as I thought about everything. Maybe this life wasn't so terrible. It was always too much work, and no time was given to us for our own endeavors, plus the occasional abuse. But, I had Locrien, and Neila, and Ondri. Maybe all my risk would net the Syrenni nothing, and I would lose the only good things I had. There was little chance that my attempts would mean my sisterhood could break free, but an increasingly high chance that I would be executed for what I had done—if caught.

I lost myself in a reverie about Locrien as I brewed capuli.

What I wouldn't give for a cup to share with him and some time to laze around and worship each other's bodies. But it was always hurried, and only at the end of a long rotation when the rest of the castle inhabitants were sleeping. Yet still, it was something, even if it wasn't entirely real—or honest. Perhaps I shouldn't be so quick to ruin what I did have.

A clatter across from me tore me out of my mental wandering. I looked over just as Ondri fell to the ground, and clutched at her chest. I rushed to her side, in an attempt to catch her before she impacted on the ground. I managed to soften the landing slightly, but not enough.

"Ondri! What is it?"

She gasped as her gills let out a weak puff. She raised a shaking hand to me, I held it as she tried to focus.

"Naiya."

My name barely escaped her lips.

I leaned closer, and blinked tears away as I felt her withering before me. "Ondri! Ondri, please-"

"Naiya, listen to me. I should have done more, to protect you and Neila. To make things better for our sisterhood. I…"

She trailed off as I searched her face. Her eyes started to turn a milky white. "Please do not Fade Ondri! I need you, we need you." I traced the countless lines etched in her face with my fingers, healed scars from Umorfae brutality in her early cycles.

"Before your maeder died, I worked to free us. But I stopped after we lost her. You and Neila needed me. And now, the Fading is upon me. I failed. I was there for you two. You are both my greatest pride. But I was not there for our sisterhood." She shuddered, and struggled to breathe as I held her. "I see the spark...in you. The same that I had. Do not let that go, it is a gift. Use it. Promise me that you will."

Her hand went slack in mine. "No Ondri! Do not Fade!"

"It is my time, young one. The Fading calls. Hopefully the next realm will not be as harsh to our kind as this one."

One last breath sighed out of her, as her membranes slid closed. Within moments, she started to disappear and shrink into nothingness. I cried out as I was finally left holding her now empty clothing.

I sobbed and sat on the ground as I held her garment to my chest, the tattered wrap that she wore every day since before I could remember now reduced to threads.

I clenched my eyes shut, when the summoning bell tolled.

No. I just wanted to sit, and cry for my lost den maeder. She had always been a solid presence, had lent the sense of safety in a wholly unsafe situation.

It rang again, louder this time.

I snapped my head in the direction of the stairway to Opius's room. Anger boiled in me as he demanded I serve him. *Culus Umorfae.* Serve him his mane fare, complete with *our* eggs, cooked by *us.*

I uncurled my fists, then put her wrap around my shoulder, before piling covered plates onto the tray. Grunting as I lifted the laden platter, then balanced it, I made my way back up to deliver it. *I will serve you, you faexhead, and then I am going to do exactly what I told the Ignisfae I would do.*

When I entered his study, I was relieved to see that he was not in sight. I placed the tray down on the smooth marble table, then backed away to rush back down to the tunnel system. I wiped a tear that had escaped, and took a breath to steady myself. As I spun to exit the door I nearly ran into Silvanis's solid form.

"Naiya, where are you rushing off to?" He asked, with his lip curled back in bemusement.

I blanched as I looked up at him, stunned. "I...I was heading down to the laundry, to begin work there. Is there something I may assist you with, my Lord?"

He pierced his steely gaze into me, forcing me to avert my eyes down to his talons. I shrank, waiting for his response. The look he had given me had a spark of something I couldn't place. Was it mischievousness? Did he know something secret, and was taking every ounce of joy in dangling it over me? He couldn't possibly know about what I had already done with the Ignisfae, I would be dead already. Or perhaps he was just in a mood and was feeling like torturing me.

At last he said, "The laundry again? Do be careful this time. Perhaps wash this old rag while you are there." He flicked an edge of Ondri's wide scarf, I had to fight against flinching at his rough motion.

I pulled the shawl closer as I held back tears. "Do not dare talk about Ondri's shawl that way," I blurted. My eyes welled as my face hardened at him. There was no way, *no way* I would let him say anything like that so close to her Fading.

The smack to my face came before I even saw it coming. Silvanis's backhand stung my cheek and sent me into the wall in an instant. He stood over me as needles pricked my skin from the sudden violence. I kept myself from cupping my cheek to soothe my smarting wound. Instead, I stayed stock-still as he glowered at me.

"Insolent Syrenni," he growled. He lifted his hand like he was going to strike again, I didn't let myself falter at all as he wound up. I would be brave. I would take it. He couldn't scare me. Not now that I was *definitely* going to do whatever I could to undermine them.

"Deliver a tray of food to the main table for me." He dropped his hand and stomped away, leaving me to suck in breaths after the heated exchange. I almost couldn't believe I had stood up to him, even if it was only a little. I smiled to myself as I rose. Someday, those damnatus Umorfae were going to get exactly what they had coming to them.

I entered the culina and glanced to where Maeder Ondri had spent her last moments, on the floor of the cluttered cookery. She had spent so many cycles toiling behind a hot stove or kneading dough from the grain she had hand-milled. I had never asked her what she had done to earn the scars, but clearly there was much I didn't know about her, and now would never know. She had traded her goals of changing our fate for Neila and I. I had never known that, not consciously anyway. I shook my head and returned to the present, I needed to deliver Silvanis his food so that I could then see to my task, the only task that mattered at this point; getting the heil out of this castle.

Luck was on my side at least, one of the kitchen servants had prepared a platter in anticipation for another Umorfae demand. *Seasoned with poison, I hope?* I bowed my thanks as I rushed the tray off to the dining room. The room was empty as I laid the heavy platter down. I left in a hurry. Had I seen Silvanis, I would have had to stay there until he excused me. It would have also been another opportunity for him to mete out more punishment for my behavior. Another drop of fortuitousness in my favor.

Finally free of my duties, once I was sure no Umorfae eyes could see me, I raced down to the lowest level of the castle. As I passed the laundry, I found Neila working.

"Neila, I need to speak with you." Her membranes flashed as she took in the shawl draped around my shoulders. I held back tears as she went rigid. I straightened my back as I approached her. "The mantle has been passed to us, sister. Maeder Ondri has Faded, I was there to ease her into the next realm. We are on our own now. She spoke of you, of her pride in us both."

Neila shook her head and crushed her eyes shut. "No, Naiya! What are we going to do?"

I stepped to her and took the shawl off. "She asked that we do what she could not, and that is to rattle the chains our sisterhood is bound in." I looped the covering around her shoulders, adjusting the fit just like Ondri always did, then caressed my sister's cheek. "I must go and see to her directive, I need you to cover for me. I will be gone some time."

Her eyes widened. "What does-"

"No, you cannot know. You are safer not knowing. But know this, I *will* fight for us, I *will* make change. The Syrenni will swim free again."

I turned without another word and headed for the underground waterways. I dove into the open tunnel system as soon as I was close enough. Swimming was the core of my being. Syrenni had to submerge in water often, we had a physical need to swim.

But the spiritual, emotional aspect that gliding through water fulfilled, it was more of an indistinct need. Part of me suspected that perhaps if we swam enough, we could undo the Taming. That would require my sisterhood to be more aware, for the veil to lift from their eyes so that they could see.

CHAPTER 8

I reached the opening while my mind waded through my thoughts. I braced for the light to impact, as I shot out of the hole and sailed down to the river below. Just as before, I wove through the obstacles at stunning speed on memory alone. My vision would not adjust for another few moments. Fortunately this time I managed to propel myself through the water with little incident. The jetty I had impacted last time I avoided, and pushed myself faster as my vision cleared.

The Ignisfae waited in his usual spot as I approached. "Greetings, Syrenni." His deep voice comforted me. "Come, we must hurry. There is a Petrafae waiting for us. At the Well."

"The Well?" I blinked as he mentioned the sacred shrine. All creatures revered it, the Maeder Tree at its center was believed to be the source of all life in Alternis. And a Petrafae! To see one of the noble Fae who had been so roughly unseated from their former stronghold, my stomach dipped in anticipation of what sights such a creature *and* the Well would be.

"Yes, I will explain when we arrive," he answered, only his eyes shone through his wrapped head.

"I have never been there, is it far? I do not know if I can walk the distance."

"It is. I thought that if you agreed, I would carry you and run. That would be the most efficient way," he stated.

I hesitated, this sounded like it would take more time than expected to do whatever it was that he was planning.

"We have this one chance, Syrenni. We need to take it."

For Ondri, for us all. "Yes, I agree. Carry me," I said as I squared my shoulders. He was right, we needed to take the chance. Ondri would want this. I could not let her down.

He nodded once and strode forward, with one motion he picked me up and slung me across one shoulder. I watched the river shrink in the distance behind as he took off at a rapid pace, racing through the trees toward the holy Well.

I lost track of time as we continued on, the buzzing energy in the surrounding forest thrummed. It heightened my sense of urgency, it felt like the whole forest was watching, aware.

My skin was cracked and drying when we finally reached the Well. The Ignisfae lowered me to the ground as I saw it. My breath hitched as I beheld the enormous tree growing out from the center of the luminous liquid, its fibrous roots glowed in a rhythmic pattern. The pulses emanated toward the tips, where tiny drops of energy wriggled out and flitted outwards in a bursting array. I turned slowly in awe, as a form emerged nearby.

I shrank back momentarily before I realized what she was. I had never seen one before, but I had heard of their striking tawny skin and rich auburn hair. It fell past her hips in a blaze of bright copper. I was still staring at her when the Ignisfae spoke.

"Syrenni, this is the Petrafae that agreed to help us. She has traveled far to lend assistance. Look," he pointed down to a conduit running from the tree across the bottom of the Well, and into the side of the wall, "that is the Imperiductus to the Umorfae stronghold. She can grow a vice around it to clamp off their power. But Petrafae are not good swimmers, nor can they stay under long. She needs assistance to get down there so she can do her work."

"What will this do?"

"I believe it will draw Opius here. With the power cut off, as he is Generalis there is no doubt Celestine will send him here. And, I would guess that the Vale Born will join him. Once they are on their way here, that will be my opportunity to strike, and separate them. I need the Vale Born to right an injustice, and furthermore Opius having a Vale Born on his side would be very bad for Alternis."

I nodded and took a breath, trying to steady myself. I stepped over to the Petrafae, her lanky legs nearly reached my eye level. I worried her height would prevent me from swimming her efficiently downward. I poised at the edge of the Well, the call of the liquid inside of it was intoxicating, I jumped in without another thought.

The sensation against my skin was unlike anything I had ever felt. The cracks that had opened from drying out on the journey healed instantly. Deep inside me, something sparked and sent a shockwave out to the surface of my body. I closed my eyes at the reaction, the spot in my core pulsed in rhythm to the surging energy of the Maeder Tree. I ran my hand over my abdomen as a tremor ran through. Whatever the fluid was resonated with me from that central point. I wanted to float in it, revel in it, as the pulse from the tree echoed inside me. I slipped through the volume as it gloved my body. Ondri flashed in my mind as I glided. Had she ever felt something so pure, so powerful? Was she afforded the chance to come to the Maeder Tree, just once as least? No one should be prevented from visiting this sacred place. The injustices to my race compounded as I realized what the Umorfae had kept us from. Presiding over our lives with hatred and contempt, they furthered the wrongdoing by keeping us from such a profound experience. Only the splash I felt behind me reminded me of what I was supposed to be doing. I surfaced to see I had gone a considerable distance without realizing it.

I resubmerged and propelled myself toward the Petrafae, who struggled to kick her legs at the Well's edge. I looped my arm around her waist. Though thin and fit, being nearly twice my size made it an effort to reach under her completely. Her ears were pinned back with worry, I could tell she was extremely uncomfortable in water. But this wasn't water. The closest thing I could think to describe it would be liquid magic. I could see now how the Umorfae must have unseated the Petrafae from their palace, they must have used their fear of water against them.

I gave her a small smile to comfort her as she adjusted gradually. She seemed to trust me a bit more and relaxed as I pulled her out further. Not having a grip on the wall sent her into a panic again, I reached up to smooth her hair in a calming motion. "It is okay, all will be fine, I have you," I said in a soothing tone.

Her breath shuddered as she looked at me. She nodded and motioned with her chin toward the Imperiductus. "We should complete our task as soon as possible." Though I gathered she was more trying to convince herself.

"Take a deep breath," I instructed. She gulped what I considered to be enough air, so I pulled her down.

It took longer than I expected to reach the bottom. The brilliant azure fluid was thicker than water, and took more work to swim through. As we reached the floor she wasted no time and pulled the rock around the conduit. Two shards of stone grew up and began to arc over, before she wriggled frantically. She required more air—immediately. I pushed us off from the base of the Well and fluttered my legs and fins as fast as I could to reach the surface.

We broke through to open air, she gasped and panted as I held her. "Not done," she choked, "not done yet. We have to go back. I could not close it in time."

I looked to the Ignisfae, standing guard on the shoreline. He indicated there was no immediate threat. Still, we had to hurry. I needed to start my return trip as soon as possible. Once she regained herself, I motioned to her to prepare to go back to the bottom again. A few breaths in, and I pulled her back. This time I pushed faster so that she would have more time to finish the vice before she ran out of breath. I watched as the vice continued its arc around the luminescent cord, then clamp down to squeeze it shut. She flung her hand at me, signaling that it was complete and she wanted me to return her to dry land.

I pulled her upwards with all my might, we broke through to the sounds of shouting. The Ignisfae motioned furiously at the edge of the Well. I swam us over to him, he whisked us out in one strong movement.

"You must go! Umorfae are nearby, but they have not spotted us yet," he hissed a whisper at the Petrafae. He slung me back over his shoulder, as I watched the Petrafae female dart off in the other direction.

CHAPTER 9

We raced through the forest at an alarming speed. Each stride jostled with an uncomfortable jab to my gut. I squeezed my eyes shut, as he ran us through the trees. At last, I scented the water not far off.

He slowed to a stop and lowered me at the river's edge. "Be well, Syrenni. If this does not work, meet me again in seven rotations."

I nodded, then turned to dive into the stream. *Over one half rotation already.* I was in extreme danger of being found out, unless Neila had been able to cover for me. I pushed myself to the limit, and swam at an untapped speed to return to the last place that I wanted to. To the place that, hopefully, my kind would swim away from and never look back.

Free.

I slipped ascending the rocks to the opening at the base of the sheer castle wall. A sharp sensation clenched in my low belly. I wanted to cry out as I shimmied up the remaining slick stone. Near the entrance, I couldn't give up yet. I hauled myself up and into the aperture, tipping over sideways into the water with a splash. I breathed a sigh out my gills as I made my way through the network to my room.

I returned with the pain steadily increasing, an ache throbbed in my abdomen. I had spent considerable energy to swim the distance both ways—and more guiding the Petrafae down to build the vice—it was perhaps understandable my body would now voice its protest. As I made my way through the tunnel system, the pain only got worse. I needed to return to my bed, to get some rest. Some submerged sleep and I would be right as the river.

I slid at last onto my sleeping platform, but peace would not come to me. Waves of intense cramping coursed through my body. They quickened in pace until at last, I cried out as I pushed hard from the inside out. I gasped and closed my eyes, afraid to look down.

I had nearly passed out from the expulsion of energy I did not have, when I heard my sister rustle behind me. "Neila, you must help me!" I tried to keep the panic in my voice at bay as I craned my neck over at her, but it was no use. I never imagined this could be an outcome of my intrigue.

She approached cautiously, then placed a hand on my shoulder. I was still hunched over, the pain had subsided some. The worst of it was over, but now...what was I going to do now? I looked down at the product of my indiscretions with Locrien. I cradled the egg that had sprouted life, a glow flickered through the translucent surface as it pulsed in my hands. Somehow, we had managed to mate, even though our kind were inherently different. We created a child which would have no place in this world, not as the world currently was. If the Umorfae found it, there was no doubt as to what they would do.

"What have you done Naiya?" Neila's voice cried as she looked at the developing embryo. "Who is the sire?"

I looked at her with nothing less than pure fear. "You cannot know, and you do not want to know. Please, promise me that you will protect the child. I do not even know what it will grow into. This is…it is the first of its kind."

Understanding dawned on her face. For once her eyes cleared. Gone were the dull Tamed eyes. They shone with knowing for the first time that I had ever seen. I could feel her awakening, the thread of knowledge sparking to life inside her. "I promise, Naiya."

"Should anything ever happen to me, it will be up to you to carry on."

She nodded and placed a webbed hand across her chest.

I gulped and stifled back tears. Without another word I drew in a large breath before I lowered into the water, holding the precious life and ducked under my bed. I began forming bubbles in rapid succession out of my mouth, then tucked them into the farthest corner under my sleeping plank. I spent all my air before going back for more, and continued to retrieve more breaths until I had built a ring. I had never known anyone who had tended an egg, but I knew at least enough on instinct that I needed to cradle it until it was ready to emerge. I cast one silent prayer for my growing spawn; a desperate plea to sisters and goddesses lost to watch over it, before I nestled it within the buoyant circle.

I resurfaced and found Neila's grave face waiting for me. I crawled up onto the platform, then looked in her direction as I mustered the strength to say, "I must rest now, if there is anyway you can make an excuse for me that will not raise suspicion. I-"

My vision faded before I heard her response.

I awoke in a jolt, the memory of what had happened flashed through my mind. I scanned the room to be sure I was alone. I ducked under the water to check on my fragile child. I realized, as much as I desperately wanted to tell Locrien—I could not. I had to protect that knowledge, I had already committed sins against my station and could be caught for them. That deed was done—but now—the egg had changed everything. I could not continue with any of it. My embryo was now my highest priority. Thoughts raced with what I might do, could I take the egg to the exit, and beg the Ignisfae to help me escape? Neila would undoubtedly be punished severely if I disappeared. Maybe she could go with me. But, if it was not her that was punished, it would just be another of our sisterhood. I wrang my hands, and could feel the pinch of my brows furrow at the consideration of what might happen. And what will happen if they find the embryo. No, I had to leave—I must leave—it was the only way. The Ignisfae would surely help, the Umorfae would never know who had assisted me anyway.

I was resolved, I would escape and bring my egg. My new hope for a future. Once my egg was strong enough, I would slip out and disappear. And with the damage to the Imperidictus, it was only a matter of time before they noticed and Opius left—making it that much easier for me to make my silent exit.

CHAPTER 10

The summoning bell echoed through the dank chamber. Each slow toll brought a tear to my eye. I sucked in a breath and headed up to see to Opius's needs.

He narrowed his eyes as I approached, I realized I was moving too slowly, too labored. Each step took effort, walking had brought back the pain from delivering the egg. I stood a little taller as I settled to a stop in front of him, feigning strength as I lowered my eyes.

"My Lord, you have need of me?"

"Assist Lily with her attire, and arrange her hair. We have a meeting with the Empress."

My eyes widened, and I was glad that he could not see them. He would no doubt have seen the momentary fear as I realized they may already know about the interruption to their power. How long had I slept? I bowed lower, then stepped over to the door, knocking on it gently.

"Yes?" a female voice answered.

I opened the door, then entered. "I have come to help you dress, my Lady."

She asked me a string of questions while I parted and braided her hair, then applied the instaura to her eyes and lips. She truly was lovely and different looking, and the way she insisted on asking me questions about myself or my kind made me feel like—in her eyes—I had value. I could almost forgive her for enjoying herself with Opius. He had a way of tricking females into thinking he wasn't evil. I lowered my eyes at the guilt that surged. Part of me wanted to warn her about him, but I couldn't.

She smiled and thanked me as I finished dressing her. I knew what she was walking into, for the most part anyway. If the other courtiers were there, she'd need to look perfect. Even perfect, she might still be ridiculed by the jealous females. They had left the last Vale Born in tears. Of course, Opius had used that situation to swoop in and be the savior. *Such faex.*

I finished preparing her and excused myself, only to find Opius waiting outside. He must have visited the balneo, his hair shone and was impeccably braided. "Wait for us to leave, then clean her room," he ordered.

I tried not to visibly sag, I was low on energy and hoped to go back and rest. "Yes, my Lord." I made an effort not to grumble the words at him as I turned to head into the nearest alcove. I knew what the orders meant: hide myself until they were gone, then continue working. Keep up the pretense, don't let her suspect how treacherous he was.

After they departed, I let myself back into her room. I looked at her messy bed and wanted to flop down on it face first. I didn't like sleeping out of the water, but I could make an exception for that enormous bed, its pillowy softness promised a respite for my aching body. However, it would only take one errant scale found in the blankets for me to be reminded of the rules and where, exactly,

I stood in the hierarchy of the castle.

Instead, I worked at changing the sheet and adjusted the pillows. Exhaustion kept me from working with any speed or efficiency. I collected everything that needed washing and headed out the door. Right as I left, I heard them returning. *So soon?*

He spotted me and motioned to the alcove. I held back my groan and did as I was silently told, concealing myself in the nook before Lily saw me. She was too busy looking at a stone in her hand to notice me anyway. *Magna, now I have to wait until he dismisses me again.* My knees wobbled as I stood, waiting for her to enter the room.

I debated leaning against the wall, when he reappeared. His monumental figure darkened the tight space I was tucked into.

"Pack a bag for her, whatever she will need for several rotations."

I schooled my face into calmness, though inside I trembled with a mix of emotions: fear, excitement, worry, hope. They crashed together like the meeting of multiple rivers, the waves colliding in a chaotic current. I hazarded a question, only one, in the off chance I may be able to determine if it was for what I prayed. That our plan worked, and he would take her to the Well. "A bag?"

He stilled, I could sense his gaze boring into me as I kept my eyes lowered. "Yes, for an excursion. Prepare appropriate clothes for a march of four to five rotations. Attire that she can comfortably walk in so that she does not slow us down too much. Let her rest for one twenty-eighth rotation, then get her up and dress her."

Four to five, four to five. I calculated in my head, with the slow pace on foot, it was conceivable it would take that long to reach the Well.

I nodded once, he turned on his heel then stomped to his rooms. My mind raced as I dashed down the stairs to procure a suitable sack and gather the clothes from the laundry.

It worked it worked.

Opius was leaving, and he was taking Lily. This was our chance, I cast a prayer to whatever of the remaining gods that might have watched over me that the Ignisfae would be successful. That he could safely separate her from Opius and change our fate. It had a greater chance of benefiting the Ignisfae, but even a slim chance it would also help the Syrenni was worth the risk.

I stuffed garments into a cloth knapsack, anything that might fit comfortably and be relatively unrestricting. I stopped by the culina and reached to grab a knife for her, but paused my hand before grasping the handle. If I armed her, she could potentially injure the Ignisfae if she fought back, but then, what if Opius was the greater threat to her? The disappearance of the other Vale Born had left an uncomfortable thought in the back of my mind. Opius had seemed self-satisfied after he returned from when she left the castle, but I never had the feeling that she left to return home. In truth, I didn't know. But something about it gave me a grim sense that it was not in her favor.

I stayed my hand, then left the culina. I couldn't arm her with a weapon, but perhaps I could give her a warning, just a small one. Hopefully enough to plant a little suspicion of Opius. It was all I could offer her and without giving away too much.

CHAPTER 11

I didn't have enough time to rest, but I did have time to stop by my Syran room. I dropped the pack and headed down to my watery chamber, then dipped under the submerged board to glimpse my fledgling egg. I funneled a few more bubbles around it, to support its burgeoning weight. I marveled at the faint glow, and the budding creature inside. I lifted my hand to cradle it from below. As my palm grazed the surface I felt a tremor, and an echo within me. It resounded off my Untamed thread, the portion of me that wasn't controlled. The lifeform pushed toward me, and caused a strong current to ripple through the water. My eye membranes flashed as I nearly gasped.

An Untamed female. With Umorfae powers over water.

I stared at her for a moment as it sunk in how truly special she was. The Umorfae would think her a mutant, abhorrent and beastly. Some of their gene pool mixed with Syrenni. To them there was probably nothing worse. But I knew the truth. Here was a creature that was a gift from the Maeder Tree, given life so that she could exist *to be* different. And thereby effect change.

I realized, as I held her, that I couldn't teach her anything about controlling water. She would have a skill that I could not guide her in. If I were to escape with her, there was no one on the outside of this castle that would help with that. But perhaps, there was one inside that would be ultimately motivated to teach her, as her faeder. I couldn't keep her a secret from him, not now. We had created a miracle together. I knew in my heart that he would never hurt her. I had to tell him, and had to convince him to join us in our escape, that we might raise her together and teach her both ways.

But first, Lily. I needed to tend to her, and tell her what little I could. I cast another prayer for my child, one of protection and luck, before I left my room, then walked down the hall to pick up her loaded pack.

I still had not rested, my fatigue held at bay with the thought of what might be. It bolstered me to carry on, to complete what must be done before I could hope to leave these dreary walls.

I slipped into Lily's room and helped her dress for the trip, then pushed the pack into her hands. I nearly blurted out more than I intended, but I had to remind myself, she was not Syrenni. My history with Opius was inherently different from her. I hated him, hated Silvanis, but she had little reason to think so lowly of them. He had shown her exactly what he wanted her to see, the glimmering exterior of immaculate, considerate behavior. There was no way she could have known the truth, even if I had told her outright, she may not have been able to believe it. No, she would have to experience it for herself.

I barely remembered what I said to her as I rushed away from her room. My mind was already in motion as I went the opposite direction from where I should have. Instead of returning to the laundry, or the culina, I turned toward the wing of the castle that housed the Praetors barracks. I needed to find Locrien, and convince him to join me. It was a risk, a considerable one. If that was too far over the line for him, perhaps he would finally out me to his superiors.

I reached Locrien's room, and made my entry the usual way, quiet and without notice. As I closed his door I saw his silhouette in the dark, waiting for me on the bed just as before. I breathed a sigh, I hadn't known if he would even be in his barrack at this time. "Locrien, I do not have much time. I have something important to tell you, and to ask of you." My heart thundered as I walked toward him. He stood, but said nothing as I approached.

"Locrien?"

"Welcome, Naiya," a voice hissed with contempt.

I retreated a step, as I gaped at a face which I could only barely make out. The one thing I could see was his gleaming canines as he stood before me.

Silvanis.

He closed the distance and grabbed me by the neck, lifting me off the ground with ease.

"Come to slide further down your descent of treachery?" His voice slithered into my ear. "How much does Locrien know? Or worse, how involved is he?"

My blood went cold as my mind raced for an excuse, an answer. Something.

"Nothing to say for yourself? No pathetic attempt at a feeble lie? I know you have been leaving the castle. And now, what have you gotten yourself? Caught for your traitorous ways. Once Opius returns, he will deal with you. And Locrien, if Opius has not already figured out his involvement, and metes out his punishment while on their excursion."

As I hung there choking, his words sunk in. '*If* Opius has figured out'...I realized Silvanis hadn't told Opius before he left. And further, Locrien was with Opius. He must have been selected to join. Had it been Silvanis who assigned him the role, so that he could trap me in Locrien's room?

With one forceful shove, Silvanis threw me backward into the wall. The sound of my skull striking a hard surface echoed through my head, as what little light was in the room shuttered to black.

CHAPTER 12

I awoke parched, dry, and aching. I cracked an eye open to sneak a glimpse at where I was. I expected to find myself in the standard Umorfae dungeon, where perhaps all Syrenni end up at some point in their lives. Sometimes it was just a short stint, to reprimand poor behavior and to scare us back into line. I myself had been incarcerated three times, each incident had been an overreaction to something small. But there were no fellow Syrenni in nearby shackles. And there were no Imus Praetors, the lowest ranked Umorfae that usually lorded over the detainees. I was not housed in anything familiar, the barren solitary cell didn't even have a water pail. I pulled my legs underneath me to rise, and cringed at the persistent throb in my head.

Faex, that hurt. I rubbed my temple as I crept over to the door. Lights danced in my vision as I neared the only opening. I peeked out over the narrow portal, placed too high for me to see anything without attempting to climb up a little.

Not a Fae in sight. I was alone. Abandoned here. Thrown in this cell with no Praetors nearby. As I glimpsed the empty hallway, I knew this was different. This was not like my previous time in captivity. But then, my whole life had been in captivity, how would tightening the walls around me be that much different? Still, I shouted to the outside, to see if any Syrenni were near me. My increasing need for water insisted I try and get someone's attention.

"Salvé? Hello? Is anyone there?"

A voice called out from nearby, out of eyeshot, perhaps next door. "Greetings," a female voice answered.

I paused at the response, I had never been privileged to such an inflection; honeyed and wise. It sounded like no Umorfae I had ever heard speak. It carried a sense of warm strength that I clung to, as I gripped the cold stone door. My mind tried to place her tone, as I thought about all the discrepancies of where I was now. "Do we await tribunal here? I have never been in this prison."

She huffed a laugh. "No, young one. This is where they put the prisoners they are ashamed of, the ones that will have no trial. They keep us here, until the need serves them, or until we Fade. I myself have been here...well I do not know at this point. Many cycles. Many, many cycles."

"Cycles?" I blurted. No, how could I be in this dreadful place so long?

"Yes, cycles. You learn patience, if you stay that long. And you learn to use any little scrap that comes your way. But no matter how long you are here, do not let it wither your resolve. They may have trapped you, but try as they might if there is something in your mind they want, they cannot have it unless *you* give it. They are incapable in that regard, never forget that. You are the master of your mind, and that gives you power."

"Why are you helping me?"

"I have no reason not to. If my helping you prevents the Umorfae from getting something they want, then I am that much more motivated to do so."

I stilled. "Are you not an Umorfae?"

A door down the hall slid open and halted our conversation. My heart was in my throat as footsteps approached. I backed away from the entrance as they settled to a stop on the other side.

"Food," a brisk voice grunted.

He slid a tray through the opening, then the sound of another platter scraping against stone echoed as he delivered one to my neighbor.

I frowned at the plate, just one old fish and a cup of water. Still, any water at this point was something. It was enough for a drink and a partial wet down of my scales. I swallowed the fish and drank half the water, then smeared the other half on myself as best I could.

I slid down to the ground and finally sobbed. The Umorfae was gone, and only my neighbor would hear. I had to let it out, at least once. My egg was alone, Neila would have to care for it, the likelihood that I would ever meet my child had dwindled to zero. I had gambled, and lost. Now she was left to grow untended, at least until Neila figured out to step in—hopefully she would realize soon that I had been taken. It may take longer for her to become aware than if I had been in the usual dungeon. Wherever I was in the castle now was well away from any chance of Syrenni gossip.

The rotations dragged on as I sat, and waited. Sometimes the female spoke to me, words of encouragement, of strength and faith.

I wondered, how could she still be so resolute in her will to live on? Why had she not let go and Faded? It was clear she would continue to sit here, stuck in her cell for an eon—if they kept feeding her and giving her at least basic needs. But who would want to rot for so long? What was it that kept her going for all the drawn-out cycles that she waited? Hope must have been a powerful companion to keep her soldiering on for all that time.

She was mid-sentence when she halted. A moment later, I heard what stopped her. Footsteps thudded, fast approaching toward our prison block. I scrambled away from the door as a figure came into view. Only a glint of opal hair was visible for barely a moment, before the lock slammed open. The door swung inward and revealed Opius's scowling face.

He was upon me in an instant. He snatched me from the ground and lifted me up to his face.

"What have you done?" He shouted a hair's-width from my face. "She is gone! By the time I tracked the Vale Born she had been caught by Ignisfae! That culus prince took her, and I know you had something to do with it. Speak!"

Prince?

I spotted Silvanis, lurking down the hall with a satisfied smirk on his face. I realized as I looked at him over Opius's shoulder, he had known ahead of time, yet waited for Opius to leave before cornering me in Locrien's room. I understood at that moment, he had also waited to tell Opius anything, he had known long before. His comments about Locrien, his mysterious glance before Opius had taken Lily to meet the Empress. *Silvanis knew, and he didn't tell Opius.*

I opened my mouth to say something, to lie at least, when my neighbor howled with laughter. It echoed through the chamber as it continued to roll out of her.

Opius whipped his head in her direction, like he could see through the walls. "Shut your mouth, you filthy harpie! And you," he turned slowly back to me, "I discovered your little intrigue with Locrien. He admitted to me the things he told you, the snippets of information you stole to use against the Umorfae. He has already been executed for his crime. His death is on *your* head." He pulled something out from a back pocket and tossed it between us. I was only able to shift my eyes low enough to barely glimpse what it was. A long bound mass of opal hair, stained with blood.

Locrien's hair. They had shown him his dishonor by cutting his hair before beheading him.

I wanted to shriek, to cry out and clutch at the pain in my chest. Beautiful Locrien—the faeder of my child—was gone. The hope of escaping with him had been dashed the moment I awoke in this cell. But now, the knowledge that he no longer lived sent a spear through my heart.

Silvanis moved closer, revelling in the microexpressions of grief I found impossible to mask. It all ebbed away. In one instant, I was emboldened, stronger. "You think Locrien was the only one subverting you? What about this one? Silvanis *knew* I was sneaking out of the castle, and *knew* of my relationship with Locrien. Silvanis knew I had compromised Locrien. Did he ever tell you, even once? I knew he was withholding that information, did you? What is *his* angle at keeping silent about such a severe threat?"

Silvanis backed up a step, his face absolutely betrayed any lie he might concoct. With his free hand, Opius unleashed his broad fist, backhanding Silvanis so forcefully that Silvanis smacked his skull on the wall. "I will deal with you later, stupid culus," Opius hissed at Silvanis.

I bit back a smile at the much deserved—though not enough—retribution.

Opius continued with a deadly quiet whisper as he turned back to me, "Since you are such a fan of schemes, I now have one of my own. I noticed Lily's softness toward you. You are coming with me, to hunt her down and take what is mine. And then I will show her, and you, who truly holds the power in Alternis."

I tried to wriggle away, but as my prison mate continued to laugh, it triggered her words to play in my head again. *You are the master of your mind, and that gives you power.*

She was right, it was the only thing I had now. The knowledge I held gave me dominance. I could not—*would not*—give it away.

I tightened my resolve, I wouldn't show fear, I would not let them win. They may have taken my freedom, long before they had thrown me in jail, but I could still triumph over them. They took Locrien, the only one of them with any merit or honor, but they would not get this piece of me. All I had now was the knowledge of what had begun, what had truly started to tear at the Umorfae foundation of control. They didn't know that it wasn't just about the Vale Born anymore, it was the life growing within their very walls, amassing power even before emerging. I knew now, she was the one. The one that would change our fate and return the Syrenni to their rightful place in the world. A fresh kernel of hope ignited in my mind. I smiled to myself, in spite of the tragedy of Locrien, of my life, of Maeder Ondri, of any Syrenni that went before.

It would all be righted one day, when my filia took it all back. And made them pay. Pay *dearly.*

She was the one.

His lip curled as he inspected me. "Why are you smiling?!" Opius shouted.

I opened my eyes fully to him for the first time in the many cycles that I had served him, unafraid, unwilling to cower any longer. I did not blink once, nor flinch as he shook me again.

I smiled wider as I said, "Hope."

ACKNOWLEDGEMENTS

First and foremost I want to thank and acknowledge my husband. With a life together full of children and chaos, having a partner that I have so many shared interests with—including cg art, story and character development—it makes life inspiring and interesting on a daily basis. Thank you, Kirt, for all you do to help everything in our lives keep moving forward in spite of the daily obstacles and constant logs thrown into our path. For the many years we have been pushing forward together, thank you for all of them. They are beautiful years that I cherish and look forward to many more with you, my love.

To all of my friends that have cheered me on, supported me, and have been there to high five successes. You are all so rad and I appreciate you! Laura, Robyn, Alison, Nikie, Meg, Jackie, Chris, Dev, Hilda, Liza, Luke, Juan, Jeff, Hunton, David, Mike, Christina...and so many more. I appreciate the many people that populate my life and bring all the positivity and support I could ever hope for.

To all my fellow Gnomonites I met when we were but fledgling cg spawn, thank you for the years of inspiration. You are all immensely talented and furthered my love and understanding of storytelling, both visually and in written form. Go on being rock stars, you've all earned it.

My brother, Evann Zilka, thank you for your support and encouraging talks and texts. You have always been there for me, and shared a deep love of entertainment since our childhood. Be it having entire conversations strictly in movie lines (while outsiders watch, very confused and very concerned) playing video games, and analyzing dialogue, scenes, or entire movies.

Once again, Laura L. Hohman, I owe you inexhaustible thanks. You have given me solid, usable notes times after time, and have been there to support and encourage me like none other. I value our friendship immensely, your skill as a writer parallels the person you are as a friend to me. You are so incredibly talented and I'm privileged to know you and be a part of your journey. It never ceases to amaze me how much you can and do accomplish. The very definition of Lady Boss, you are the absolute best and I adore you!

Chris Sanchez, thank you for beta reading, and giving me your honest and helpful feedback. Thanks for being my friend and compatriot in this easily cringeworthy process of spilling one's brain on the page. A friend in writing is a friend indeed.

David Martin Lins, my brother in storytelling and my esteemed, keen-eyed editor whom I rely on and respect. Thank you for your insightful feedback, your helpful notes and careful catches you make in my work. I don't think I can sum up in one paragraph how much your comments on what I write mean to me. You have the most wonderful balance of sending notes, along with praise, jokes, and more notes. The notes improve my work, the jokes make me laugh, the praise bolsters my confidence. You are the editor that every writer deserves to know, and the writer that every reader deserves to read. Talented to no end, I am honored to know you.

Lastly once again, to my parents. Jay and Carla Zilka, you are wonderful humans that have taught me so much, and continue to do so even though I am now grown and with children of my own. You've shown me how to exist in this world, and to keep learning; that there are always more avenues to pursue and learn from, regardless of age. The world is brimming with knowledge, there is no shortage of it, there are only more opportunities to learn and grow. I learned that from you both, and learned that the more we know, the more we realize there is to know. Thank you for being a strong guiding gale of a wind, that has brought the ship that is my life steadily along its course—even with the jigs and jags along the way as I discovered who I was and where I might land in this world. When I figure it out I'll let you know!

Thank you for reading! If you enjoyed this book, I'd be very grateful if you posted a short review. Your support really does make a difference, I read all reviews personally and use them to keep bringing you great stories. Thanks again for your support!

Get updates on release information, exclusive giveaways, and insider info by signing up for my newsletter at www.lorinpetrazilka.com